FOR EVERYONE
WHO HAS EVER LOVED

*Love is a very big idea. Love is a very powerful
feeling. Love is something special and sweet and simple and sacred and
love is best when it is shared. The more love is shared
the more it grows, the further it reaches, and the greater it becomes.*

*Thank you for this opportunity to share my love with you.
Please feel free to share it with others.*

*Love,
Dallas*

An Awesome Book of Love!

Copyright © 2013 by Awesome World LLC

All rights reserved. Manufactured in China.

For information address HarperCollins Children's Books, a division of HarperCollins Publishers,
10 East 53rd Street, New York, NY 10022.

www.harpercollinschildrens.com

Library of Congress Cataloging-in-Publication Data is available.

ISBN 978-0-06-211666-6

12 13 14 15 16   SCP   10 9 8 7 6 5 4 3 2 1 ❖ First Edition

AN AWESOME BOOK OF LOVE!

BY DALLAS CLAYTON

HARPER

An Imprint of HarperCollinsPublishers

IF I WAS A DINOSAUR

IF I WAS A RIVER
AND YOU WERE THE SKY

IF I WAS DOWN LOW
AND YOU WERE UP HIGH

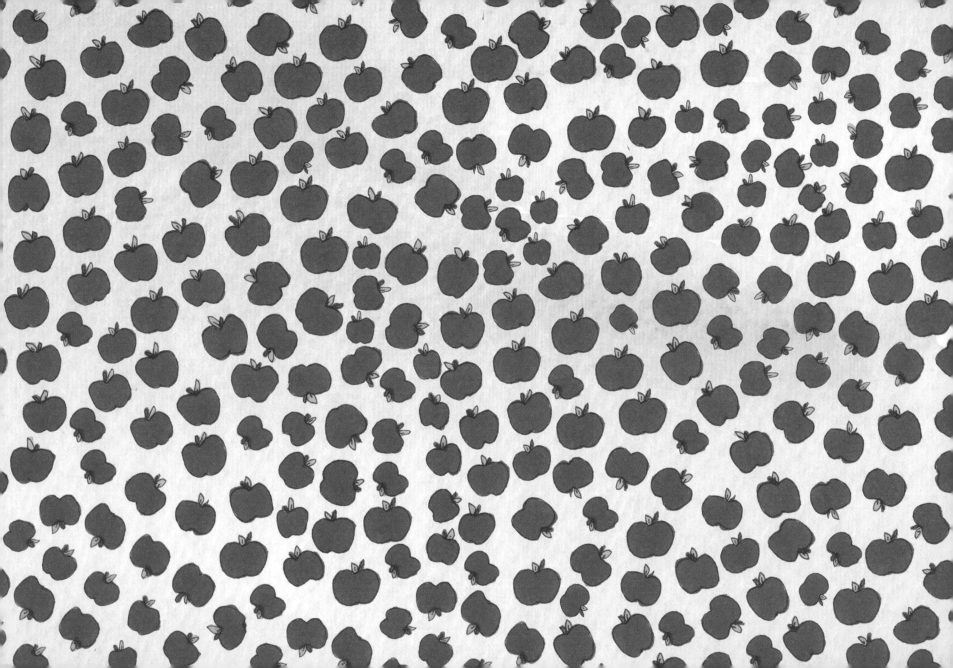

OR IF I WAS AN APPLE
AND YOU WERE A SUNDAE

IF YOU WERE A WEDNESDAY
AND I WAS A MONDAY

AND I WAS
THE FALL
WE MIGHT NEVER
HAVE
GOTTEN TOGETHER
AT ALL.

AND WE'RE AS TOGETHER
AS TOGETHER CAN BE

AND YOU KNOW
I'M AGLOW
WITH A SMILE ON MY FACE
WHEN I WONDER
WHAT MAGIC
YOU'LL MAKE OF THIS PLACE
OF THIS TOWN
OF THIS WORLD
YOU'LL TRANSFORM YOUR SURROUNDINGS!
THAT SPIRIT INSIDE YOU
IS TRULY ASTOUNDING...

AND WHEN I'M BESIDE YOU
I'M LEAPING
AND BOUNDING

SO PROUD
I CAN HARDLY
CONTAIN MY HEART
POUNDING

I LOVE

I LOVE

IN SO MANY WAYS

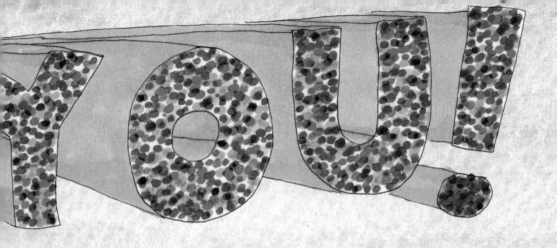

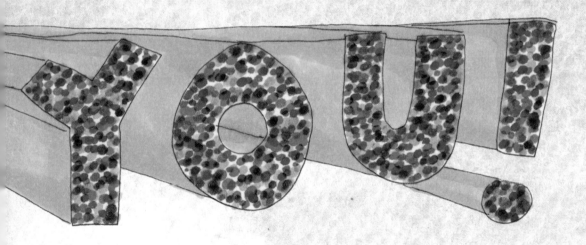

OVER THOUSANDS OF YEARS

OVER BILLIONS OF DAYS

AND DANCE LIKE A FOOL IN
THE COLDEST TOWN FOUNTAINS

I WOULD PAINT IT ON WALLS
IN COLORS SO BRIGHT
THAT THEY'LL GLOW IN THE DARK
WITH "I LOVE YOU" ALL NIGHT

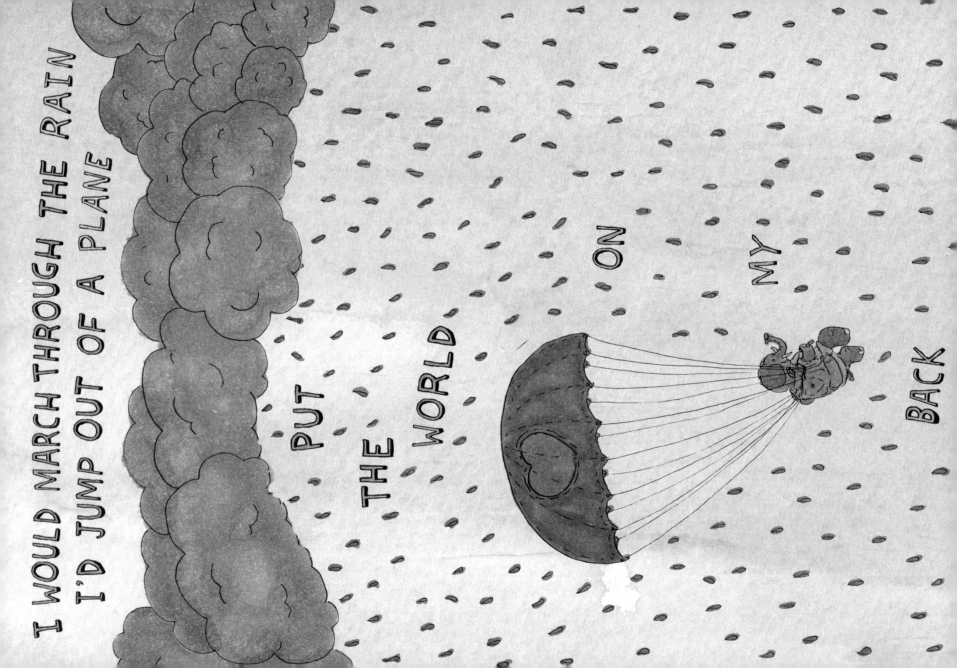

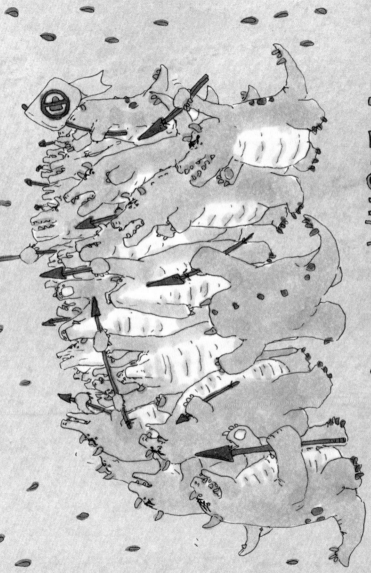

I'LL STILL RACE DOWN A TRAIN

AND I'LL STAND DOWN WHOLE ARMIES DEFENDING YOUR NAME

BUT YOU KNOW
THAT'S NOT ALL THAT THIS LOVE IS ABOUT

SOMETIMES IT'S A WHISPER
WHEN YOU FEEL YOU COULD SHOUT

OR JUST
BEING AROUND
WHEN THE OTHERS
HAVE GONE
OR ABOUT
LETTING GO
WHEN YOU WANT
TO HOLD ON

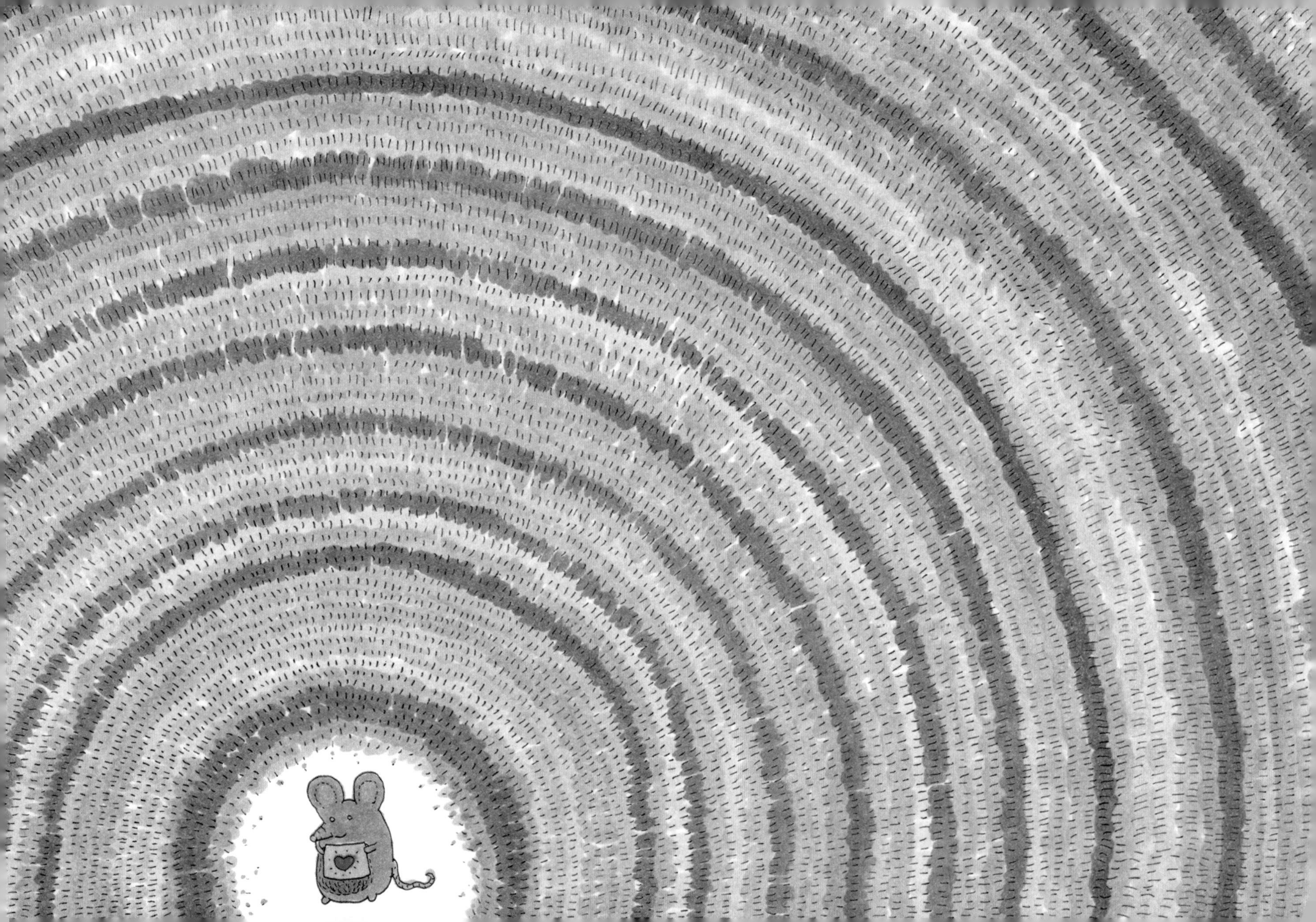

IT'S ABOUT LIVING LIFE
   WITH SUCH STRENGTH AND EMOTION

AND KNOWING THAT WAVES
   ARE JUST PART OF THE OCEAN

JUST
LIKE
THE LOVE
THAT HAS BROUGHT US TOGETHER

WHEN I'M HOLDING YOUR HAND

WHEN YOU'RE MAKING A PLAN
WHEN YOU'RE THINKING A THOUGHT
WHEN YOU'RE DANCING A DANCE
WHEN YOU'RE JUST HANGING IN
BY THE SEAT OF YOUR PANTS

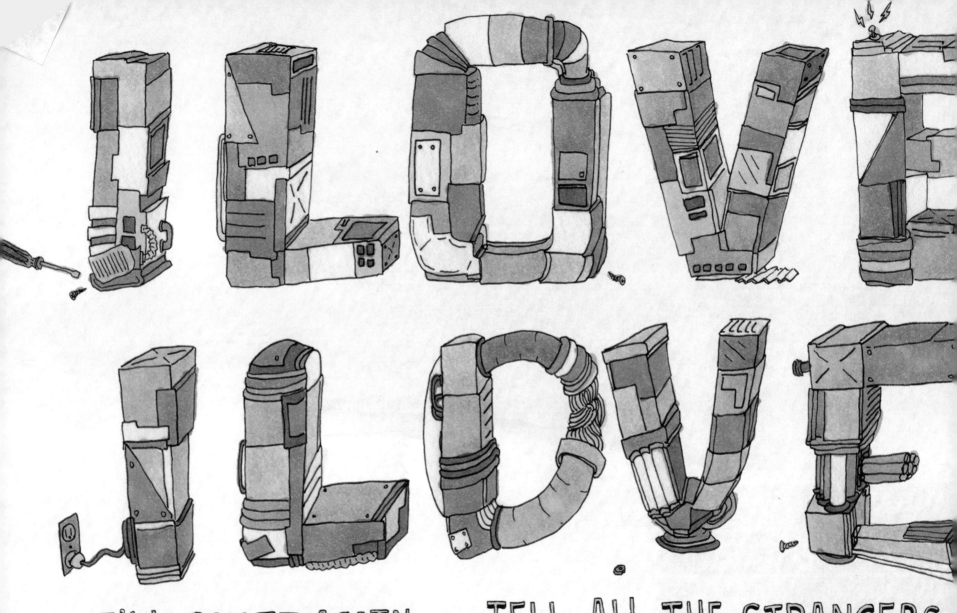

I'LL SAY IT AGAIN   TELL ALL THE STRANGERS

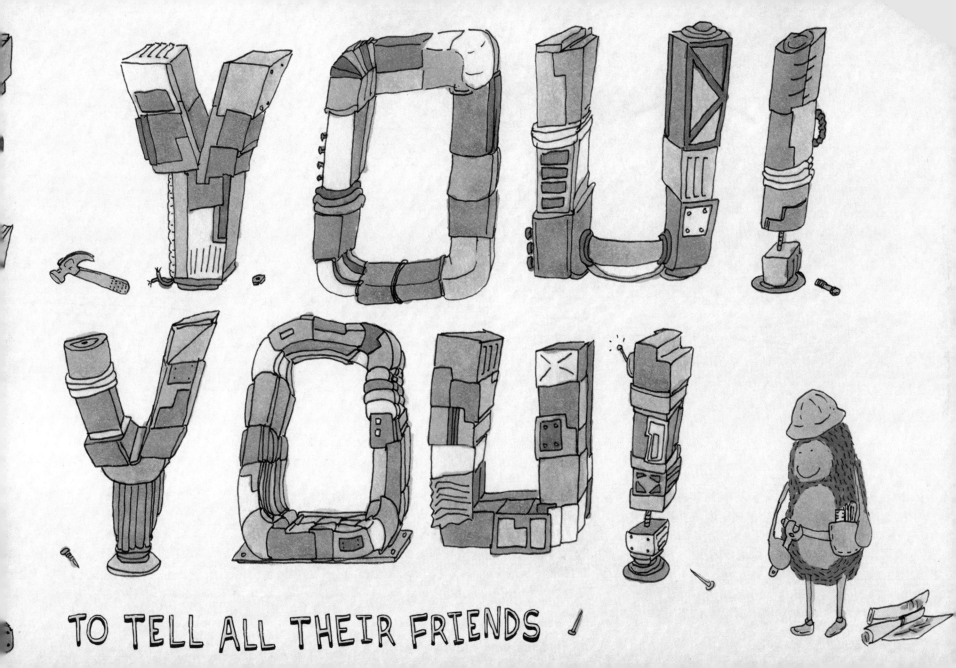

YOU! YOU! YOU! YOU!

TO TELL ALL THEIR FRIENDS !

MAKE IT A SONG
AND WE'LL ALL SING ALONG

I LOVE YOU!
I LOVE YOU!

YOU MAKE ME FEEL STRONG

YOU MAKE ME FEEL
YOUNGER
YOU MAKE ME FEEL
BRAVE
YOU MAKE ME
FEEL SOMETHING
THESE WORDS CAN'T CONTAIN

ND IF YOU WERE THE FUTURE
AND I WAS THE PAST

IF I WAS TOO SLOW
AND YOU WERE TOO FAST

IF YOU WERE A CLOUD
AND I WAS A GHOST

IF YOU WERE LONG DISTANCE
AND I WAS UP CLOSE

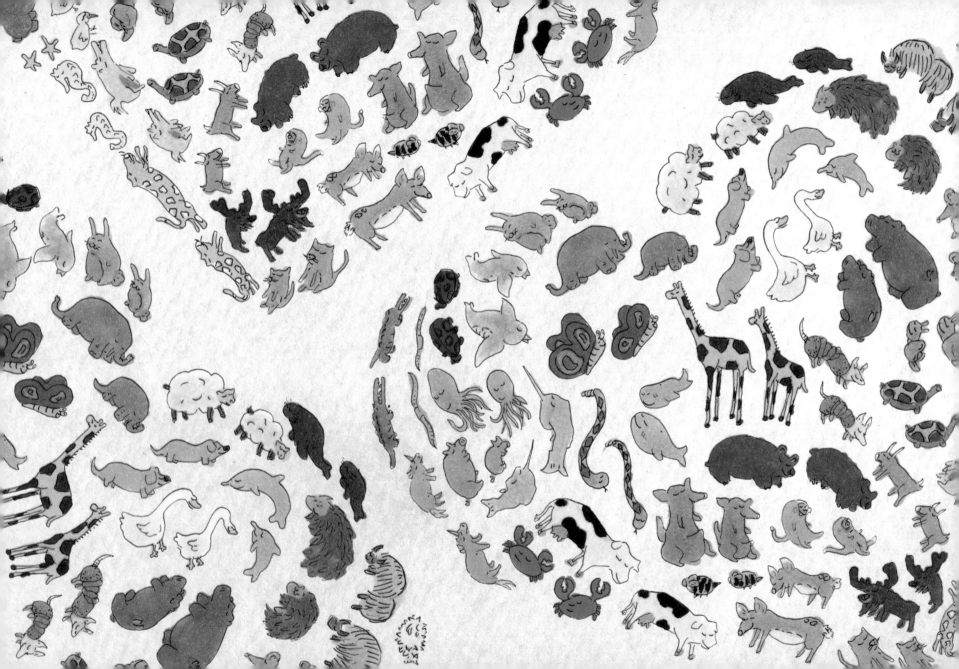

I'D STILL LOVE YOU
NO MATTER WHAT SENSE
IT WOULD MAKE
I'D LOVE YOU WHENEVER
WHATEVER IT TAKES
I'D LOVE YOU NO MATTER
'CAUSE YOU'RE YOU
AND I'M ME

TOGETHER FOREVER
IN LOVE AS CAN BE.

THE END

DALLAS CLAYTON
IS A WRITER
ILLUSTRATOR
AND CREATOR
OF ALL THINGS
GOOD!